XAVIAN, BENEATH IT ALL

A Swordsfall Lore Book

Brandon Dixon

Swordsfall Studios

Copyright © 2020 Swordsfall Studios

All rights reserved

The characters and events portrayed in this book are fictitious. Any similarity to real persons, living or dead, is coincidental and not intended by the author.

No part of this book may be reproduced, or stored in a retrieval system, or transmitted in any form or by any means, electronic, mechanical, photocopying, recording, or otherwise, without express written permission of the publisher.

Illustrations by Enmanuel Martinez, Jonah Lobe and Tumo Mere
Map by Brandon Dixon
Cover Design by Taylor Ruddle

Printed in the United States of America

CONTENTS

Title Page
Copyright
Foreword
Chapter 1 | How Tikor Was Born — 1
Chapter 2 | Xavian — 8
Chapter 3 | The Wretched Ones — 17
Chapter 4 | Raksha — 27
Chapter 5 | Xavian's Touch — 35
Chapter 6 | The Massacre of Ghinor — 45
Chapter 7 | Adume — 58
Glossary of Major Terms — 63
Chronicles of Tikor — 65
Books By This Author — 69
About The Author — 73

FOREWORD

Every hero needs a villain, right? Well, in Swordsfall it's more like a whole host of villains huddled around an ancient being. It's easy to call Xavian evil, but is he? Or is he carrying out a natural sense of order that's just deadly to humans?

I love a good existential evil, and Xavian fits the bill perfectly for Swordsfall. I wanted to add a real dark sort of energy to Swordsfall. One that was completely inhuman. Yet something smart. An entity that knows how to play on the worse of humanity's tendencies.

-BRANDON

CHAPTER 1 | HOW TIKOR WAS BORN

"How Tikor Was Born" is a classic fairy tale about the origins of Tikor and Ishvana's great sacrifice for her children.

A very, very, very long time ago, before the world even existed, there was a great being of kindness and compassion named Ishvana. She roamed through The Great Cosmos, enjoying the sights and sounds of the hollow universe. One day she came across a huge river of life called the Etherforce. Ishvana had seen this phenomenon before but never one so big!

The kind supreme being decided that, here on this stream, she should create a new world, one of magic, beauty, and splendor. So Ishvana eagerly began building a gorgeous planet that she would fill with life and love.

A Perfect Little Planet

Etherforce flows through all living things, and placed upon a river of Etherforce, the planet could support lots of life. Thus, Ishvana crafted a great, big world where many amazing things would live. She carefully thought about what to call her finest work of all. Then, a name popped into her head: Tikor, which means "beautiful planet" in her ancient language. Finally, when the world was just right, she created her children on Tikor, the Divine Entities.

As deities of the new world, her children were mighty like their mother and capable of creating life, for Ishvana had passed down that gift. Ishvana and her children lived happily on Tikor. That is, until a stranger appeared.

Darkness Arrives

What Ishvana didn't know was that by creating Tikor directly on the Etherforce, the planet's life sang throughout the Great Cosmos. The current of life carried the joyous sounds far and wide until it landed in the ears of a vile, corrupting supreme being, Xavian. The Corrupted One slumbered as he drifted the cosmos. He had already devoured everything he knew existed, so when the faint sounds of Tikor drifted through the Ether, the Corrupted One awakened in hunger.

Xavian followed the happy sounds until he finally found the young planet. Ishvana sensed his approach, but it was already too late.

The Withering King had arrived.

Battle For Tikor

While Ishvana embodied kindness and compassion, Xavian was the manifestation of loathing and malice. As the Master of Decay, his very essence brought about corruption, and his arrival caused the seas to churn and the ground to heave. The Withering King was destroying Tikor with his mere presence. Ishvana, eager to protect her children, began to battle against the Corrupted One. But supreme beings like Ishvana and Xavian don't fight with bodies, they fight with the very space and energy around them. Time stopped and started; planetary bodies were created and crushed. Ishvana's children could only watch as their mother fought Xavian. With the two supreme beings evenly matched, their battle for control continued.

However, Xavian, the master of corruption he was, had a plan up his sleeve.

The Second Sun

Xavian realized how much Ishvana loved her creations and decided to use them against her. As The Withering King's presence slowly corrupted Tikor with each passing moment, his corruption eventually seeped deep into the world, which allowed him to steal some of the newly birthed nature spirits and elementals. Xavian then crafted a second sun and imprisoned these spirits within, essentially holding them hostage.

The concerned Ishvana didn't want to risk killing the kidnapped elementals by destroying the solar prison, but she refused to stand idle. The Great Creator tried bargaining with the mad god, but it was no use. Xavian didn't come there to talk, though he entertained her pleas to stall Ishvana, allowing his corruption to spread further—for his sinister plan to finally hatch.

Then with a great sundering, the sun prison erupted, and horrifying winged creatures came pouring out. Xavian had corrupted her children into The Wretched Ones: powerful, destructive dragons of nature driven by a primal fury.

Nightmare Creatures

The winged beasts surged through space toward Tikor with a ravenous hunger for its fertile soils. Ishvana, as sad as she felt for her lost children, had no other choice but to destroy the beasts. Yet, try as she might, she couldn't since these corrupted creatures—Xavian's trump cards—were born of her own energy. The great dragons finally landed on Tikor, annihilating all that stood in their way, with only the Divine Entities able to oppose them.

The dragons were extremely powerful, as they had both the magic of Ishvana and Xavian. Even the Great Creator's firstborn children couldn't stand up to the beasts' raw strength. Moreover, the mother goddess could not help without turning away from her lethal opponent. All seemed lost when a miracle happened. One of The Wretched Ones, Ryuujin, defected and joined Ishvana. Xavian was furious, for Ryuujin had been one of his most powerful creations. Ishvana had pulled a trick from the Corrupted One's own book and turned it on him by purifying Ryuujin with her light.

With the great dragon on Ishvana's side, the tides started to shift.

Ishavana's Sacrifice

Even with Ryuujin's help, the conflict wouldn't end before the world reached the point of no return. No barrier could fully withstand the corruption that Xavian emits, and The Withering King wouldn't stop until he had destroyed Tikor. So, the Great Creator did something only she could to save her planet—she merged with the Etherforce flowing right through Tikor.

With that huge energy boost, Ishvana swept the land with Ether, repelling Xavian's corrupting energy. Then, using the last of her power, she created a dimensional wall between the energy of the Divine Entities and Tikor's plane of existence. This act sealed Xavian and his corruption into its own dimension, saving Tikor; however, it also expelled supreme beings like Ishvana and Xavian from Tikor, leaving only the world's deities and the creatures the Entities had created.

With the cosmos safe from Xavian's corruption, the kind and gentle Ishvana faded into the Etherforce, joining its infinite energy.

Better World

With Xavian gone, Tikor could finally heal from the scars of its long battle. The land had forever changed; this once sterling, beautiful, and perfect world had become imperfect. However, it was also filled with abundant new life, gifted by the gods with powers they needed to survive.

With Xavian's energy contained, The Wretched Ones were greatly diminished and defeated. They couldn't be destroyed, so they were entombed deep below Tikor, where no one would ever find them. While saved, Tikor's inhabitants will always need to watch out. Xavian, The Withering King, remains just Beneath It All, awaiting his moment. Though as long as Tikor's loving children remember the Gentle Creator's sacrifice, all life continues to flourish among the stars.

* * *

Variations Of The Story

Not everyone in Tikor agrees with this version of the planet's origin story. While one of the most commonly referenced genesis stories, various cultures have decreed this rendition as biased. The two main groups that believe and propagate this version are the Karu and Dracon, the two ethnic groups behind Tikor's two biggest nations.

The See'er - This esteemed group of oracles believes a much different version of Tikor's origins. They uphold that their divine entity, Ro'og, created the planet.

The Lucomi - In the desolate southern region known as the Outskirts of Vinyata, the Lucomi are far removed from the influences of Vinyata and Garuda. They view their omnipresent god, Odu, as the Great Creator.

CHAPTER 2 | XAVIAN

Beneath It All holds a dark and calculating god. Sealed from the physical plane of Tikor he lurks, waiting for his moment.

# XAVIAN, BENEATH IT ALL

It's hard to imagine why any sentient being would willingly create an entity as maleficent as Xavian. If a supreme deity had such power, why construct something so destructive? This line of speculation has caused many on Tikor to believe the sinister god originated from something else, from somewhere else. That perhaps, for example, The Withering King was born from an unnatural set of cosmic events.

Several researchers have even suggested that Xavian appeared from the void itself or, more absurdly, was created at the heart of a black hole. Ultimately, Xavian's origins are just as unclear as those of the creation goddess Ishvana. While the citizens of Tikor celebrate Ishvana for her strength and kindness, Xavian is a dark cloud that hangs over the world, ready to rain cruelty on the globe at any moment's notice—a mighty essence that revels in devouring the cosmos.

A New Toy

The various creation myths totally agree on one thing: Xavian waited for the next world to destroy. He seemed content to drift among the cosmos until the smell of purity caught his attention. One day, an eon ago, the Corrupted One sensed Tikor. The creation of the planet had been so successful for Ishvana that the waves of positive energy beamed its existence across the galaxy, a grand and joyous beacon to the universe.

Xavian received that message loud and clear. The newly-formed planet became his new target, an unfamiliar toy for him to play with. The Withering King came to tear Tikor apart at the seams, corrupting the world's core bit by bit while slowly savoring each step,.

> *Do you think knowing about this will help you? Does truth protect you from the Lion? Can you defend your throat with the thin shield of Knowledge? Can you?*
>
> — WHISPER

God Vs. God

When the dark god arrived at the freshly created Tikor, he liked what he saw. The mother goddess Ishvana stepped in to defend her creation. For mortals, it's hard to imagine a battle between titanic powers like the Divine Entities. Deities such as Cadmus have explained their clash as a fight between pure elements, two colossal storms heading toward each other with frightening power.

Perhaps Xavian had the edge in the fight. For him, there was nothing to protect. He didn't have to split his attention; he could strike like a spear at a singular point. By its nature, corruption is slow, steady, and effective. Xavian, too, exemplified all those qualities, holding his own against his cosmic rival while waiting for an opening: the moment when Ishvana must try to handle two fronts. When that moment finally came, The Withering King sprang into action, setting off a chain of events that would be etched into Tikor.

Corruption's Power

A battle between equal powers often ends in stalemate or worse—the death of both participants. Xavian didn't desire mutually assured destruction, the corruption deity had a more insidious plan. Instead, the opportunistic entity seized the first opening he had, swiping a cosmic hand at the planet. His aim wasn't destruction, but a simple abduction instead. The Elementals of Tikor had piqued Xavian's interest since his arrival at the planet. The raw bundles of personified elements made an excellent canvas for him to paint his horrors.

No one on the planet knew what powers Xavian had at the time, but they soon learned. The Withering King thrust the Elementals into a second sun of his own making, Adume, entrapping them in the womb of a pulsating star that warped the Elementals with its foul energies. When the prison sun later cracked open, it didn't release the primal spirits of Tikor; instead, Adume unleashed winged horrors that the world would come to know as Dragons.

Sealed Beneath

Xavian surely meant for his twisted dragons to tip the battle in his favor, and at first, they did. The party of dragons descended on Tikor, causing destruction and untold damage to the fledgling planet. But, the Master of Decay had underestimated how deeply Tikor had imprinted on the Elementals. The former Earth Elemental turned dragon, Ryuujin, betrayed Xavian after the world itself seemed to call to him.

Ryuujin's betrayal tipped the balance toward Ishvana, but it wasn't enough. Xavian is corruption incarnate, and his very presence affected the world. Despite Ryuujin returning to Ishvana's side, the theft of the Elementals had still given Xavian an advantage. Animals of all kinds were birthing abominations; the weather was changing. Xavian pushed the world toward the brink just by existing, so Ishvana made a desperate sacrifice in order to save her planet. The Great Creator bonded with the very Etherforce force that flows through Tikor, using the energy to create a barrier across Tikor and to seal Xavian in a separate dimension.

Alone In A Void

The Divine Entities are beings of supreme power. Even the Withering King did not foresee the actions Ishvana would take to end the war. Trapped on the other side of a dimensional mirror, Xavian could only watch as Tikor's defenders thwarted his invasion. The Wretched Ones were dispatched one by one, most of them by being sealed in tombs around the world. The monsters he had inadvertently spawned were hunted down. His corruption waned as his influence was cut off.

The seal that holds The Withering King is of unparalleled power. For a time, it proved the end of Xavian. With his presence sealed, Xavian's name faded from the mouths of humans. He was no longer the ever-present danger. Perhaps even the Divine Entities themselves forgot about the Master of Decay as their focus shifted to the planet's struggles. His silence didn't mean his surrender though. It merely signified his eternal patience while he awaited his chance.

> *You sit in your homes and think you're safe. Do you feel safe? Do you sleep sound at night? Or do you worry? Do you wonder? Does my name ring out in your mind after a*

nightmare?

— WHISPER

Tear In The Wall

They say a space is only a prison when a person gives up. Xavian isn't a person, and he doesn't give up. The empty space of void was nothing at first.

It only held Xavian.

That was Ishvana's mistake in her sacrifice. In the same way The Withering King had underestimated Ishvana and her resolve, so had she and his decaying presence. Tikor was protected completely from his influence, his touch, and his power; however, the realm he was trapped in was not.

So while the world forgot about him, Xavian molded the space into his own palace of corruption. As Tikor's guardians and heroes dispatched his creations, accidental or not, those corrupted creatures' malignant energies needed somewhere to go. Tainted with his presence, his Ether, they couldn't return to the great Etherforce stream that Ishvana had bonded with. To complete the cycle, their energies were drawn toward the one place that would accept them: Xavian's realm.

The dark place Beneath It All.

As humanity tinkered with life's forces, their mistakes punched microscopic holes in the wall separating them from the Corrupted One. Not a breach in the seal, but a cosmic loophole.

The Long Game

Each poke from a botched spell or cosmic event provides a window for Xavian. He whispers to Tikor from the peepholes through the veil, exploiting the ignorance of anyone foolish enough to listen. His plan is unclear, but the number affected by Xavian's Touch increases every year. Each infection becomes a possible vector point for fiercesome voidbeasts, the Raksha.

Spirit Mediums warn that the Raksha and the Touch aren't the only methods Xavian has to influence Tikor. Just because the world hasn't heard about other methods doesn't mean they don't exist. Corruption never sleeps; Xavian never sleeps. There are talks of cults bubbling up in the corners of Garuda. The dead congregate in the wastelands of the Ebon Cascade. A Dark Spiral looms deep in the waters of The Grand Divide.

Meanwhile, the fallout from the Genesis Explosion and the death of Mime still reverberate throughout Tikor. The gods can die, yet Xavian remains. The balance of Tikor seems uneven, and only two things are certain: Xavian is patient, and corruption is slow. The world has yet to see his full plan.

The Agents Of Chaos

The Wretched Ones - The first creations of Xavian are still the most infamous. The exact number of dragons created is unclear. The Elementals were a primordial force—some known, some unknown—yet all The Wretched Ones were defeated in the ancient battle for Tikor. Or at least, that's what the gods say. If all of these great dragons were sealed, will they remain secure? If one besides the traitor Ryuujin exists, why has no one heard from them? If they are free, what could they be doing?

Xavian's Touch - This combination of disease and curse is a sickness that can never be eradicated. When times are hard, humans can't help but fall low. The Touch awaits opportunities when dismayed minds lack protection from the gods. The odds of a person falling into a Raksha's possession are extremely small, yet the threat alone causes towns to alienate any individual thought to have it. Xavian's Touch keeps the dark god in the minds of humans, which, in a way, only leads to more infected.

Raksha - It's unclear where these awesome beasts of horror came from. Researchers and Hekan users both say the creatures are supernatural. Unfortunately, known Raksha events are so rare in history that they provide no insight, aside from the fact that the Raksha bend to Xavian's will. Where there is the Touch, there is always the distant threat of these bloodthirsty monsters. The most disturbing thing about the Raksha is that they their supernatural abilities remain unknown. Only their immense strength and unmatched viciousness is known

Cults of Decay - No government on Tikor will admit to having Xavian cultists in their mist. Records tell of the gore-soaked conclusion that was the first, and last, Cult of Xavian. However, mankind does not learn easily from one bad outcome, and the voice of Xavian is a seductive one. It remains possible that some individuals don't know who they are in spiritual bed with. They might have touched the altar of a corrupting god without evening knowing it. One can only wonder what kind of havoc could be unleashed by Xavian's unwitting human allies.

Predator Morals

Most people assume that being aligned with Xavian

means having no morals, though this lies far from the truth. Xavian himself has a sense of morality that can be observed through his curse and creations. One can only assume that a being of Xavian's level would also possess the ability to create life from Ether.

Yet, he never does. He only takes; he only corrupts. The Withering King's morals are that of a predator. Never creating, only taking. When he couldn't take all of Tikor, he didn't just give up. Instead, Xavian settled on picking off the denizens of the world. Even if he has to do so one by one.

Philosophy Of One

Those who try to follow Xavian or fall to him have a simple philosophy: selfishness in its purest form. The single pursuit of satisfying one's self. From the Raksha who drown themselves in the pleasure of rending flesh and shedding blood, to The Wretched Ones who went to a place of their choosing to spread their chaos. Each of these creatures were set free to follow their convictions.

History has never spoken of those punished by Xavian. His agents do as they please, as Xavian has empowered them to do—the ultimate philosophy of pleasing your deepest and darkest desires. No matter the cost.

CHAPTER 3 | THE WRETCHED ONES

Once glorious Elementals, they were morphed into horrifying dragons after being abducted by Xavian.

When the planet of Tikor was first created, it was alive in its own way. The Elementals are a direct reflection of the planet's will. Ishvana didn't create the aspects of nature, rather they came from the world itself. Invokers often talk about the difficulties of channeling the basic properties of the world, a task easy on paper but harder in execution. It's almost hard to imagine a time when such invocation was effortless.

The Elementals enabled a level of magical freedom that made the creation period of Tikor so fruitful. Much debate continues over whether the Elementals were a response to the world's growth or if they were responsible, much like ethereal gardeners tending to a garden.

Unknown Spirits

The number of Elementals is hard to ascertain despite their prominence in tales. The deities that have spoken about this early historical period admit that even they don't know of all the Elementals. The world was growing and changing at every moment, with new life springing up constantly.

Humans untrained in the arts of Hekan often think of the elements when they hear Elemental. This presumption paints only part of the picture, as these base elements like Fire and Water were elementals—but also Sky, Earth, Time, Gravity, and others. For each inconceivable part and rule of Tikor, there was an Elemental. Together with Ishvana's children, they combined forces to develop the planet.

> *In some ways the period of growth for Tikor ended the day the Elementals were lost. It didn't destroy the world, as you can see, but it stunted its growth. There's no telling what things would have been like if we had power of that magnitude roaming the world.*
>
> —JALEN OF ANCIENT HISTORY

Abduction By Decay

None of Tikor's inhabitants knew how much everything would change when Xavian arrived, for he was an entity that they couldn't have dreamed of yet. Ishvana didn't even have the time to warn her creations of the power that the Corrupted One possessed. When The Withering King shifted his gaze to the planet and its Elementals, they were all exposed.

With a swipe of a cosmic hand, he abducted the budding lifeline of Tikor, its Elementals. The corruption had a simple goal: to steal the lynchpins of the fledgling world and corrupt them. The only thing he enjoys as much as destruction is corruption. Xavian crafted the second sun called Adume and encased the Elementals in its intense energies, thus warping them into something else—something Xavian could control.

Birth By Adume

Adume served as more than just a prison. It was an enormous cosmic oven that baked the primal energies into something different and foul. Some of the gods say that they felt Tikor howl, as if it were aware of what was happening to its children. Ishvana tried to release her planet's children from their cage but to no avail.

Still locked in a cosmic battle, Xavian never allowed Ishvana to interfere with his star's dark design. It's unclear whether she gave up or was just stalled long enough, but either way, the Elementals were lost that day. When the sun Adume split open, it became clear that nothing would be as it was before.

Awakened As Monsters

When Adume cracked open, it brought about a terrifying revelation. The innocent Elementals had transformed into brutal dragons which became known as The Wretched Ones, each of them monstrously sized and seemingly ready for battle. Some emerged with enormous wings and tails; others had razor-sharp fangs and other bestial qualities. Their abilities as Elementals often fueled their new and dark powers—an affront to what made them special on Tikor, as they became the planet's greatest enemies from that moment on.

The dark energies of Adume had purged whatever personality and essence of Tikor they had, reprogramming them into thralls under Xavian's control. Now soldiers of The Withering King, The Wretched Ones had little choice but to follow his orders.

Descent On Tikor

Xavian wanted The Wretched Ones to pursue a simple goal: the destruction of everything keeping him from his objective. The gods and spirits of Tikor stood in his way, and along with Ishvana, their meddling only served to slow him down. Xavian tired of this exchange and sent his powerful, warped abominations back to Tikor. All those connected to the Etherforce were his enemy, so The Wretched Ones set down on Tikor to decimate their master's foes, the dragons' very essence altering the world as they walked across it.

The sun-born brood fell upon different parts of Tikor, taking on the world's defenders wherever they landed. However, the power of each Wretched One was overwhelming in its sheer ferocity. While Tikor's defenders had an advantage in numbers with gods, spirits, and animals all gathering together to protect the planet, it wasn't enough to match the unfettered power of corrupted, raw elements.

> *My brother especially doesn't like to talk about those days. Humans wouldn't understand it, the feeling of standing up to the rawness of nature. Feeling the weight and smelling the stench of its corruption. Every day I thought it would be our last, and it wasn't. Sometimes though, I think we would have welcomed it. Anything to make the endless fighting stop.*
>
> — DIVINITY OF WISDOM, MIME, DURING A SOMBER SERMON ON THE EVE OF THE PLANET'S BIRTHDAY

The Betrayer

As the brood of dragons set to destroy Tikor's divine guardians, the difference in power came through in each fight. With the Elementals gone, replaced by their corrupted counterparts, the war began falling into Xavian's hands. However, in the Northern Hemisphere of Tikor, a pivotal battle turned at the hands of betrayal. Ryuujin, the former Earth Elemental, regained his memories and self through a rekindled connection to Tikor and the Phoenix Garuyda.

With his old identity back, Ryuujin betrayed his brood, joining in Tikor's defense; his turn was enough to halt Xavian's advance, pushing the victory further away from the dark god but not completely out of reach. Ryuujin's unforeseen betrayal had pushed the epic battle into a stalemate, one that would only last as long as the traitor dragon held the tide against two of his corrupted brethren.

Source Disconnect

Locked in a stalemate that favored Xavian, Ishvana decided to gamble by sacrificing her life to the Etherforce itself—giving up her essence to become one with life and Ether. As her last conscious act, she enacted a barrier across Tikor, protecting it from the corrupting touch of Xavian. The barrier also trapped the Withering King in a planar pocket, his own eternal prison. With Xavian sealed, The Wretched Ones' powers faded.

Since their corruption, they could no longer recharge from the Ether around them, though Ryuujin managed to function after he had reestablished a weak link with the earth. Ryuujin explained to the defenders of Tikor that the dragons couldn't be killed. The primal energies in The Wretched Ones were too strong and volatile.

Sealed For Eternity

Since the great dragons were immortal according to

Ryuujin, the Divine Entities had to come up with a new plan. They decided the only option was to seal the monstrous beasts away. Not an easy task, but one that had to be done to save the planet. The Wretched Ones didn't just surrender to their fates, however.

Even underpowered and magically restrained, the fearsome creatures caused significant harm to the ones performing the sealing rites. Howls rang throughout Tikor, as the dark energies in the dragons still simmered despite having been cut off from their source. A few screamed out curses to their captors, one of them in a language never before heard. It was as dark a day as it was joyous. The Wretched Ones did not just go quietly into the night—they fought their fate every step of the way.

The Rogues

The term "Rogue Dragon" is used sometimes when referring to the traitor dragon Ryuujin. Lately, more and more people have begun saying "The Rogues" as rumors spring of strange happenings. The exact number of The Wretched Ones never lined up with the number of tales about creatures that sounded like dragons. Strange occurrences have aligned with the ability of a Wretched One. Some people claim that those epic and violent creatures could never exist on Tikor, and many point out the Rogue Dragon as proof. After the war, Ryuujin remained fairly quiet and then disappeared later in his life. If he could go missing, why not other dragons?

The Brood

- **Ryuujin - Former Earth Elemental**. Ryuujin betrayed his brood during the battle for the Tikor. He reconnected with the earth, causing his memories to return. His whereabouts are currently unknown, as he disappeared shortly after establishing the Republic of Vinyata.

- **Yobida - Former Flame Elemental.** Yobida was once the guardian of the flames; now his twisted dark flames melt anything they touch. Defeated by the combined efforts of Ryuujin, Garuyda, and Garuyda's children, The Divinity. Yobida was sealed in a place known only to a select few.

- **Inkyaban - Former Sky Elemental.** Inkyaban once ruled the skies, showing the other creatures how to soar. Transformed into a winged horror, Inkyaban controled the weather, making the skies unsafe for all. He was defeated by Ryuujin and Garuyda before being sealed somewhere under Garuda.

- **Ayida'we - Former Rain Elemental.** Ayida'we was said to be multi-colored with a twin personality that caused her appearance and color to change. As an Elemental, the rainbow was once her symbol; after her corruption, it had been replaced with drowning waters and pulverizing hail.

- **Grootslang - Former Shadow Elemental.** Grootslang was one of the oldest primals when he was an Elemental. With enormous tusks that can cleave mountains, it's unclear where he was sealed. Some suspect the rumbling under Enkai hints at more than just the mountain god.

- **Uroborous - Former Iron Elemental.** Uroborous was once the Iron Elemental, consuming and redepositing minerals throughout Tikor. After being unleashed on Tikor as a Wretched One, he set to consume the world's resources. He was sealed somewhere in the depths of The Grand Divide.

- **Masingi - Former Harmony Elemental.** Masingi was once the Elemental that helped bring everyone together. Masingi has since become the bringer of chaos, the sound of his roar breaking down the minds of others, as weather and nature warp around him. Rumors say he was sealed in the Ebon Cascade.

- **Apep - Former Light Elemental.** Apep was changed the most out of any Elemental. Once a vibrant expression of the sun, he became the stormbringer. Where he went, light faded and despair settled in. There's no real evidence as to where he was sealed, if at all.

You think this is the end, child of Ishvana? Our dark father is only separated from us. Not gone. You don't have the power to end us, and you know it. Bury us away, little ones. Forget about us. Celebrate this victory. It'll make it that much more satisfying to kill your children when we're released, for we are the true immortals.

— YOBIDA DURING HIS SEALING RITUAL

Public Agenda

The Wretched Ones' main agenda was clear from the beginning: the destruction of all spirits and gods in the world. Not just in a general sense, but down to the very last one—until there were no more gods on Tikor. Even the dragons themselves told the gods of their intent during their epic battle. While the Wretched Ones didn't fulfill their objective, the sheer hatred they seem to carry for Ishvana's children runs deep. There's little doubt that if The Wretched Ones ever broke free, they would continue their bloody campaign.

Supposedly, where the dragons descended wasn't random either. If the primary goal of the twisted group was just to kill all deities, then why not concentrate in the North? That region hosted the highest concentration of gods at the time and would have been the optimal place to launch an assault. Yet, The Wretched Ones only sent three of the brood to the North. The epic Spirit Mediums, the Mwadi, have spoken about how the world has Spirit Anchors—points of concentrated Ether that are a highly guarded secret amongst high-ranking Hekan users.

Disbandment

While the official word is that The Wretched Ones are all sealed away, if not gone. Many people have questioned whether or not this claim is true. Given the unknown number of Elementals that Xavian had stolen, then the number of dragons must be unknown as well.

So the question is, are all the dragons truly sealed? Or like Ryuujin, could they be lying low somewhere?

CHAPTER 4 | RAKSHA

Many things are called nightmare creatures in the world of Tikor. But the Raksha are the one, true nightmare creature.

To say the Raksha are the greatest nightmares facing Tikor would be an understatement. While Tikor has many strange and dangerous animals, monsters, and spirits, none invoke the same level of dread as a Raksha set loose on the world. Alongside Xavian, the mere mention of their existence strikes terror in the hearts of many. The few times the Raksha have appeared, they often cause damage on a scale rivaling that of wars.

So where do these abominations originate? What could have created an evil so dark that its birth starts with the consumption of a human soul? The most obvious answer would be The Withering King himself, Xavian. The Raksha are often called Xavian's Children. But are they? Or are they something more?

Unknown Origins

The earliest mentions of the Raksha reach all the way back to Tikor's biggest battle, the day Xavian arrived. While the Raksha aren't referenced by name in any tales or texts, creatures from the void are often mentioned. Descriptions of terribly twisted monstrosities that Xavian summoned from a source of primordial wickedness are liberally spread throughout ancient texts.

Some scholars say that these describe the Raksha or, at the very least, the earliest version of them. The leading theory claims that Xavian is truly a corruptor and not a creator, so he couldn't have created the Raksha, but rather he corrupted someone else's creation. Believers of this theory argue that the Raksha were formed in the same way Xavian corrupted the Elementals into The Wretched Ones.

If this theory is correct, then not only do they not know what the Raksha are, but they may never know. Right now, the only truth people have about the Raksha is that they are a horror that Tikor must learn how to combat.

HAHAHAHAHA AHHHH AHAHAHAHAH!

— OBALU THE RAVENOUS AS HE MURDERED INNOCENTS DURING THE GHINOR MASSACRE

From Within

The Raksha are not born on Tikor. No, these terrible creatures come screaming and ripping from a host's body. The victim's soul is consumed by the newborn Raksha before the creature tears its way through the host. The final stage of Xavian's Touch is possession—not by a spirit or god, but by a hungry Raksha straight from Beneath It All. These creatures sit in the depths of the mirror dimension where Xavian himself is sealed. Unable to directly affect the events of Tikor, instead the Corrupted One waits and nibbles at the holes in the souls of the weary and the sad. When victims have succumbed to the curse and opened themselves to Xavian, he rewards them with the essence of a Raksha, a horrifying end to the slow mental decline caused by the Touch.

Unknown Desires

Once unleashed upon the world, the Raksha indulge in whatever defective vision of entertainment they have.

Most of these nightmare creatures enjoy wholesale slaughter and the glorious sensation of the screams of innocents on their skin. The Raksha are visible because they essentially do not care if others see them. Whatever rules society and the world has, they want to do more than just break them, for the Raksha completely ignore societal norms.

The most famous Raksha incident was the 50-year reign of Obalu the Ravenous. The fearsome creature was birthed into the world accompanied by the screams of the slain. The town of Ghinor and the surrounding woods would never be the same. After Obalu was finally killed by the combined efforts of a 2,000 member regiment of Divine Order soldiers, many questions were asked, including why a monstrous creature had the intelligence of sentient life while being solely content with the murder of humans and the consumption of their flesh.

Raksha Amongst Us

Denizens of Tikor often celebrate that the Raksha are little more than mythical beasts, the torturous prize at the end of the slide of Xavian's Touch. Given the public nature of abominations like Obalu the Ravenous, a common belief is that the world would know if any Raksha were alive right now. Unfortunately, this is not the case, though these implications are disturbing enough that the truth is rarely spoken aloud.

Spirit Mediums have warned people for over a hundred years that dark forces reside on Tikor. These warnings tend to fall on deaf ears, as no Spirit Medium these days is foolish enough to try and make spiritual contact with a Raksha. There have, however, been a number of persistent stories that lend credit to the soothsayers. Evil takes more than just the form of mindless slaughter, after all.

The greatest threats often come from enemies that are cold, dispassionate, and persistent, silently biding their time until the perfect moment to inflict maximum bloodshed. Some of Tikor's most vicious creatures across Garuda and The Republic of Vinyata have gone silent over the years, their bloody trails dried up. Locales attribute this silence to good tidings and divine protection, but perhaps these vile creatures have simply found a leader.

Aa-mire is coming. He's coming for us all. The Uncaring he is! Aa-mire is coming. He's coming for us all. The Uncaring, he is! Aa-mire is coming. He's coming for us all...

— THE RANTS REPEATED BY A SPIRIT MEDIUM UNTIL
HE DIED OF THIRST A FEW DAYS LATER

Individual Nightmares

No two Raksha are the same, as they have a diversity that rivals humans and gods. One of the leading theories poses that the Raksha in a way are the humans that hosted them, that they take on elements of the mortal coil during their birth by possession. Perhaps there are even Raksha born from animals, each morphed and corrupted in their own way.

One of the most popular urban myths about creatures, the Nandi Bear is an animal so twisted and horrific that it must have been tainted by Xavian's Touch and the Raksha. Debates over the nature of Raksha continue to rage on, as directly studying a Raksha is a fool's craft. Thus far, what little is known about the monsters comes from the autopsies of the few confirmed kills.

In most cases this knowledge rarely helps in understanding the walking horrors, for their physiology seems to make no sense. One mediciner who examined the corpse of Obalu the Ravenous famously said, "The insides of that monstrosity looks like a god closed their eyes and waved their hands." Whatever powers the Raksha have still lies outside the grasp of human understanding.

Leader Of The Damned

A man was found dying of dehydration on the edge of a small town in the Ilun Valley. The villagers helped the man, giving him water and bringing him back to life. The man started yelling. He kept repeating one thing over and over again. That Aa-mir the Uncaring was coming. Witnesses described the man as being inconsolable, writhing and twitching as he ranted. The name is foreign to anyone who hears it, except to the deities. The gods always go silent when it comes to matters of Xavian and the Raksha, with one exception: Aa-mir.

When a parishioner said the name to the Divinity of Battle Cadmus, he froze—a gesture common for humans but almost unheard of for a deity. The war god said nothing, but his reaction was clear. He knew the name of this Raksha. The unwitting messenger had all the signs of a Spirit Medium who had tapped into something spiritually stronger than himself.

The weight of the Raksha's mind crushed the Medium's, imprinting upon him and leaving him little more than a blabbering mess set to repeat what was most likely the same words the Raksha had said to him. The message seared into his brain was the last conscious thought he would ever have.

Hunt For The Source

Just as the study of the Raksha rarely yields results, they are just as challenging to kill. Tales say the Raksha have been defeated in a whole host of manners; however, records only account for Obalu's rampage, one in which it took 2,000 soldiers to destroy him. Casualties were so heavy that only five hundred remained afterward. Direct approaches rarely work on the Raksha since their power once fully born is prodigious. The point of the Raksha's greatest weakness happens before their birth.

Blighthounds have taken it upon themselves to do the job they believe no one wants: hunting down those with Xavian's Touch and cutting them down before they can reach the final stage of the disease-like curse. These powerful Spirit Mediums take the treatment of the Raksha with utmost seriousness. The spirits Blighthounds channel make them fierce and aggressive. Once they have the scent of corruption, they unflinchingly pursue their duty. Even if their target doesn't actually have the Touch—even just a hint of corruption—to a Blighthound, it's all the same. Many innocent people have fallen at the hands of these so-called protectors, so many regions in Tikor have forbidden the practice of hunting people thought to have the Touch This has not deterred the Blighthounds, and they continue their search for the corrupted, legal or not.

❊ ❊ ❊

Anatomy

The morphology of each Raksha is weird, alien, and grotesque. Obalu the Ravenous, for instance, stood over three meters talls and had arms long enough for his fingers to touch his knees. All the muscles on his upper body were enlarged beyond proportion. The blood from his victims had soaked into his skin like a sponge, creating the brilliant red coloring on his face. By every known study of animal, creature, and humanoid physiology, none of that should work together. Yet the hulking creature was real, and it had lived. Very well at that.

Genetics And Reproduction

Historically, the Raksha have never been known to reproduce. Or have much interest in the process or the human body. The only known way for a Raksha to be "birthed" is when a human gives into Xavian's Touch and accepts him. While some myths persist that the Dark Spiral, a swirling dark storm in the middle of the Grand Divide, is also a gateway to Beneath It All, those superstitions have never been confirmed. What people seem sure of is that the Raksha don't reproduce, they infect like a parasite. Devouring the host upon its arrival.

Average Intelligence

It's hard to gauge the intelligence of creatures like the Raksha. The maniacal Obalu had clearly known how to navigate the dimly lit alleys as well as how to hunt and disappear for years undetected. So the common assumption is that any Raksha can be as intelligent as the human they possessed—though most likely greater than that.

CHAPTER 5 | XAVIAN'S TOUCH

Xavian's Touch is a type of spiritual corruption caused directly by the Corrupted One, and the first step toward being possessed by a ravenous Raksha.

Xavian, The Withering King, lurks Beneath It All and always searches for ways to corrupt the denizens of Tikor. However, because of Ishvana's Sacrifice, he's barred from any direct influence, but the master manipulator has found various little ways around her grand protection spell.

All humans have free will, which also gives them the ability to give up their invisible divine shield. If a person willingly renounces deities, the protection breaks, and the Corrupted One can begin his influence.

Renounce It All

Ultimately, Ishvana's Sacrifice is an everlasting protection spell for all beings that have Etherforce flowing through them. All living creatures on Tikor are born with this innate resistance to outside influence. However, since the bulk of Etherforce flows down from the gods to the beings they created, cutting off that flow also cuts them off from Ishvana's protection. Any humans that operate at a spiritual level are aware of this intrinsic shield from harm, but unfortunately, the rest of the world is not always as informed.

Through Tikor's long history, people's faith in the deities have occasionally faltered. During those times, events in the world tested the faith of the gods' followers, and sometimes the gods did fail them. That breach of trust has led some down a dark road they didn't even know existed.

> "Be free of the shackles of constraint and normalized society. Free of the gods, free of the rules. Free of the bonds of morals, free of all limits. Eat all you want. Do whatever you want. Fuck all you want. Just be free. Free of the human vessel."
>
> — WHISPERS

Crisis Of Faith

Giving up one's divine shield often comes about for a myriad of reasons. Some are as simple as a betrayal by their deity or seeing a scene so horrifying it makes the individual lose their faith. Sometimes the separation comes from more complicated sources, such as personal traumatic events and chronic depression.

While all these things can cause an individual to verbally renounce Ishvana's protection, the conditions for Xavian's Touch are more specific. There is a level of despair that a human must reach before their bonds with Ishvana truly break. Even then, not all who lose their faith gather the attention of The Withering King.

The unlucky ones that do, though, start to hear something faint.

A whisper in the dark.

Infected

The first sign of the Touch starts with a whisper. A soft and gentle voice in the back of the mind. It faintly mixes in with other thoughts and feelings—a nudging whisper toward the more indulgent things in life. Eat a little more, sleep a little more, fornicate a little more. The voice entices through sweet seduction rather than sheer horror, one of the main reasons Xavian's Touch is so insidious. At first, it just feels like a person's mind has directed them to be happier, to enjoy life more. The voice reminds them to truly bask in the light and be free.

It's that cascade of thoughts that sets off the infected's descent into madness. Treatment is easiest during the first stage, but it's when the symptoms seem more positive than negative. On the outside, the individual is much happier than normal. Perhaps a little too happy. But few question these outward signs. Eventually, the whispers turn into something more sinister, a questioning of your reality.

> *"What have the gods done for you? Do they even care? You're having fun right now without them, so why devote yourself to them? Wouldn't it be more fun to be free? To not have the blindly devoted judge you for living your life to the fullest? Don't you deserve that?"*
>
> — WHISPERS

Mental Breakdown

Though infected, the early stages of Xavian's Touch simply prepare the host for a full connection. Giving up the protection from Ishavan's Sacrifice is only half of what's needed. To become completely corrupted, the infected must reach out to The Withering King and invite his influence. This step starts with questions regarding their lives and the divine. These probing inquiries at the back of the victims' minds slowly break them down.

The unending questions, day and night, demand answers. Demand a solution. These auditory hallucinations steadily increase in volume until a victim can no longer distinguish between their inner voice and Xavian's whisper. Before long, the murmurs begin to disrupt normal sleeping patterns and standard day-to-day life.

Inner Rage

The combination of lack of sleep and the probing whispers increasingly drain the infected. At this stage, the violent outbursts begin. They usually start as an overreaction, a snap remark at an unusually high volume and force. Then, they escalate into fits of extreme rage, where a small issue now becomes a huge ordeal.

Then, the mood swings and rage become ever more frequent and dangerous. As this stage progresses, victims start to respond to the whispers out loud, no longer able to distinguish between internal and external voices. These violent actions often lead the victims to altercations with loved ones and local enforcement. Xavian, always opportunistic, uses these instances as the final trigger—a whisper of deception from their loved ones.

> *"Why can't they see what you see? Why don't they ask the questions? Why do they always blame you? Why don't they ever defend you? What have they done for you? Nothing. You're all by yourself. You don't have to be alone. If you let me in, I can show you the answers you seek. We can have everything. Let me in. Say the name. Say my name."*

— WHISPERS

The Raksha Await

The last step to possession is the permission question. Days or weeks of slow manipulation lead up to this final junction. The point where the whisper finally asks for one thing: to be let in. To let the power of Xavian flow through them. This is the last time when the victim can be saved, a final chance at salvation. Possession by a Raksha is irreversible.

If the infected agrees and invites Xavian in, the infection completes. A Raksha begins to worm its way inside of the vessel, devouring the victim's soul bit by bit. Any unlucky onlookers witness the person screaming in primal agony as something terribly old and dark consumes them from the inside. Eventually, the screams subside once the Raksha finishes their first meal. Newly replenished from the destruction of the host spirit, the Raksha fully awakens, and the true horror begins.

Evil Returned

The Raksha are the epitome of twisted desire and pure unabashed evil. Coming across one of these dark beasts in the wild is rare; while the Raksha are among the most lethal entities on Tikor, their numbers are low. However, when a Raksha returns to the mortal plane via Xavian's Touch, they become more dangerous than anything normally seen.

After fully taking control, the Raksha warps the host body to resemble its true form. After a few short cycles, the transformation finishes, changing a previously human being into a living incarnate of hunger and carnal destruction.

> "…….*Xavian.*"

❋ ❋ ❋

Causes

Xavian's Touch is caused by a mixture of internal and external factors. Not one single thing can trigger the infection, but rather a combination of the two categories.

Internal Factors

- Fixation on negative thoughts
- Emotional trauma
- Mental illness
- Intense stress

External Factors

- Abandoning/Losing Divine Protection
- Death of a Loved One
- Curses
- Physical Illness

Symptoms

- Vivid Hallucinations
- Rapid Mood Swings
- Uncontrollable Fits of Rage
- Insomnia
- Reddening of the Pupils

Treatment

There are only two ways to cure the victim of Xavian's Touch: through ritual cleansing or ritual sacrifice.

Cleansing Rituals

Xavian's Touch is the single hardest infection or curse to dispel in known history. The corruption of The Withering King is immensely powerful, and only the strongest of Sunu will even attempt to cleanse it. As with most rituals, the downside is always having the disease-like curse rebound and infect the Sunu. With the Touch, however, the effects are so potent that there is no known safeguard from a potential recoil. The victim can only be saved within the earliest moments of infection before Xavian can convince the host to open up.

Godly Cleanse

The only other way to cure Xavian's Touch is by the deities' power. If convinced, a sufficiently powerful god can invoke Ishvana's Sacrifice and force the infection out of the victim's body. However, as with most things, it comes with a cost. The first of which is pledging loyalty to the god. A pledge of loyalty with a deity is far different than being a regular worshipper, for this agreement becomes etched in the human's very soul, making it a matter of life or death.

Prognosis

Stage 1 - Infection (whispers in your head)
Stage 2 - Host Preparation (hallucinations)
Stage 3 - Mental Degradation (rage)
Stage 4 - Invitation (Raksha possession)

Affected Groups

Adult humans are the only ones infected by Xavian's Touch. Children who have not undergone the rite of passage are not affected. While scholars remain unsure as to why, most theorize that since children are not known to the gods until the ceremony, they simply can't give up their protection yet.

Prevention

A strong and healthy community is the only sure way to prevent possession on the level of Xavian's Touch, as a robust support unit can lift others up during hard times. Individuals who start with no faith are curiously not at risk for the Touch. For instance, The Grimm and citizens of Grimnest as a whole have never reported a case of Xavian's Touch. This seeming coincidence has led most scholars to theorize that Ishvana's Sacrifice applies regardless of faith. However, having this protection and then actively losing it is the key to actually nullifying the Sacrifice.

Cultural Reception

Unfortunately, even if the victim survives Xavian's Touch, they are ostracized in most cases. Succumbing to the Touch is often seen as a sign of inner weakness—someone who can't be trusted with important duties. This treatment often leads to the victim becoming exiled, suicidal, or even reinfected.

CHAPTER 6 | THE MASSACRE OF GHINOR

The following is an account taken from a mix of personal retellings, official records, and spirit interviews from the bloody 50-year reign of the Raksha known as Obalu the Ravenous.

To this day, it remains a mystery as to who exactly was the patient zero for the birth of the Raksha, Obalu. The carnage where the rampage seemed to have started was too extreme for anyone to truly figure out who birthed the monster. In fact, prior to the night, it seemed like a completely ordinary night in Ghinor. That is, until a primal and soul-shivering howl rang out through the growing lumber town.

Witnesses say it made their blood run ice cold as a sense of horror gripped any who heard the sound. However, the noise didn't cause immediate panic or fleeing. In many ways, that proved the fatal mistake which doomed many victims that night—the failure to run for their lives while they still had the option. The best-detailed facts from that night came from the very few survivors, the ones with the sense to flee when they first heard the Raksha's screams.

The howl that signified the birth of the malignant creature came from the northeast side of town, where the carnage appeared the most severe and thus made it impossible to determine the origin point.

Failed Defense

Within the first few minutes of the initial cries of slaughter, the various guards, protectors, and such that made up the small militia of Ghinor went to investigate. According to town records, the town's makeshift defense force consisted of around 40 people. The self-proclaimed protectors of Ghinor encountered Obalu the Ravenous on the north side of town, only a dozen meters from where the howls had originated from.

It's impossible to say what went through their minds that night when faced with such a foe, but their actions were certainly commendable. The remains of the security forces were found scattered around the area, seemingly slaughtered on the spot, but their brave and short sacrifice is largely seen as the main reason the southern half of town even had enough notice for some denizens to escape. The speed of at which Obalu conducted his slaughter caught everyone completely off guard, and within the first ten minutes of his awakening, the Raksha had already murdered a couple dozen villagers.

> *It was that howl that first woke me up, even though I really didn't know what it was. It almost sounded like a large wolf or maybe even a Nandi Bear, I suppose. I do remember being more annoyed about being awoken than anything else. Then I heard the screams. It started down near Mombe's store on the northeast side. Sky's above...the screams.*

> *I recognized some of them, ya know? I've known Mika and her husband for years, even started up a shared garden a while back. I knew those voices. I heard the scream, had to be Mika, and then just silence. It kept getting closer with every new scream, and that's when I knew it was something else.*

— GHINOR RESIDENT
THE FIRST REIGN OF OBALU: THE UNTOLD STORY OF
THE MASSACRE OF GHINOR

Broken Shields

Within the first hour, Ghinor lost around half its population of 25,000. A few generations of growth erased in just an hour. The primal screams echoed throughout the town, confusing people as to where to run. Some of the voices belonged to Obalu, some of them to his victims. The laughter mixed in with the screams until they were often one. Many victims accidentally ran toward the hulking Raksha, turned around by the echo of pleas chorusing around them.

The nightmare creature was on a methodical mission of genocide, ruthlessly hunting down anything that moved. He would run full sprint down the town roads, pursuing any stragglers or people looking to see what the commotion was. Obalu moved with haunting speed, overtaking people before they could even turn to run, and impaled them on twisted spears. Then, a pair of Celestial Shields showed up. A Ghinor local had known the divine guardians were nearby and ran off to get them, and the pair encountered the monster near the center of town. Later, their shields were found cracked in half at the scene—their remains scattered throughout the mid-town area.

Empty Town

At this point in the siege, very little was known about the entity stalking the streets, aside from his hulking size and speed. The swiftness of the midnight assault caught the villagers off-guard, leaving them vulnerable. Some locals successfully fled for the surrounding woods when they first heard the commotion. Many Ghinorians simply barricaded themselves in their homes, thinking they could ride out whatever disaster was happening outside. A few braver citizens dared to defend their homes, either from inside or in small hunting parties hastily thrown together by neighbors.

No matter the reason, it was a fatal mistake to have stayed behind. This night was not one to ride out, and all those who stayed in their homes, barricaded or not, ultimately died. Obalu systemically went from home to home, breaking down barricaded doors with ease. Blood-curdling screams rang out as the Raksha impaled victims onto his sickly spears and simply ripped apart others with his bare hands. By the time the soft daylight touched the blood-soaked grounds of Ghinor, there was only one thing left alive in the town. Obalu.

Haunted Woods

The erasing of Ghinor didn't end Obalu's slaughter—it marked only the start of his reign. The beginning of a nightmare; the place where the effigy of brutality was born. The town's annihilation was an announcement, a gore-soaked statement, as its streets literally ran red with blood and the buildings dripped with gore. When traders arrived the morning following the massacre, they could barely contemplate the scene. The town was unrecognizable.

The level of death that happened overnight defied everything they knew up to that point. The bodies left behind had all been completely decapitated so that not a single human head remained in all of Ghinor. At first, the deaths were blamed on mythical Nandi Bear packs, the only native Garuda creature with murderous intentions and a taste for brains. The Divine Order of the Phoenix was called to investigate as rumors circulated about the ghost town. The investigation hit a dead-end, however, when the first witnesses and the initial traders went missing as well. At that point, reports started coming in about something in the Ghinor Forest encircling the town and nearby areas. People had started disappearing at an alarming rate.

Raksha Extermination

The uncertainty regarding what happened that night in Ghinor and its haunted woods persisted for another 50 years, though it wasn't for lack of trying. Over the years, dozens of spirit investigators, diviners, and more looked into the mystery. Many of these sleuths never returned, which only added to the mystery and hype of Ghinor. In 1505 D.A., a breakthrough happened that finally shined a light on the haunted woods.

The famous Spirit Investigator Sahar Lightdawn successfully channeled a spirit from one of the victims from that terrible night. Up until that point, no Spirit Medium had contacted any spirit from the Ghinor massacre. The trauma of what transpired made them either dangerous to the Medium or made it impossible to hold a stable connection. Sahar, with the help of a Ghinor survivor, channeled a fallen Celestial Shield who gave a sickening firsthand account of Obalu's murder spree.

The pair of Shields had been completely crushed by a hulking beast of incomprehensible strength. Only one thing in history had the power of that magnitude: Xavian's favorite monsters, the Raksha. The Divine Order of the Phoenix immediately ordered a full regiment of 2,000 soldiers to locate and destroy the voidbeast.

...As we came around the corner, we weren't really sure what we were looking for. But I think we all had assumed it would be an animal. Something large and out of control, like a starving Nandi Bear or the like. That's what the locals had screamed as they ran past us. I had my doubts, though. I remember thinking to myself, "Nandi Bears aren't from around these parts," as we turned that corner. The thing's back was to us.

And just from seeing the muscles on its huge back, I knew we were over our heads. Then it slowly turned its head around toward us, right as the thing pulled the head off of some poor man....that's when I knew we were dead.

— CELESTIAL SHIELD ATTILIAN GHILSOUTH, FROM THE SPIRIT CONFESSION CONDUCTED BY SAHAR LIGHTDAWN

Throne Of Skulls

It's hard to say if the regiment tracked Obalu to his cave or if the Raksha lured them there, mainly because of the first night the regiment spent along the outskirts of the Ghinor Forest region, where a few soldiers went missing while on patrol. A few days after that night, a soldier disappeared while relieving himself in the nearby woods. The nighttime disappearances only intensified as regiment moved deeper into the thick woods. After a week of playing cat and mouse, the forward edge of the regiment came across a large, ominous cave. When Prime Shield Malik Faye and his commanders entered the tight cave space, they knew they had entered the beast's lair.

They, however, weren't ready for Obalu's sheer size, speed, and power. The Raksha stood atop an enormous pile of skulls—the work of over 50 years terrorizing the countryside unabated. The monster killed one of the cave exploring parties before they even had a chance to react. A swift demonstration of what the Celestial Shields were in store for. When the rest of the regiment outside of the cave witnessed the Prime Shield and two other senior leaders emerge from the cave at top speed, they knew something was wrong. The howling, three-meter tall brute came barrelling out the cave, stunning the regiment. They were staring into the maw of true horror. Their greatest nightmare had come to life.

Bloody Battle

The first thing any survivor of the Battle of Ghinor usually talks about is the sheer mass of the Raksha. The word "hulking" paints a picture in itself, but when the survivors say it, they do so with emphasis. His size, not just in height but in width, had arrested the minds of many. Obalu looked strong enough to rip a tree from the ground, root and all. This strength was confirmed when he leaped onto a helpless soldier near the cave exit and ripped the young man's head clean from his shoulder with a sickening pop. His speed was uncanny, and his violence unprecedented. The first handful of soldiers died just from the sudden confusion caused by the fonts of blood spraying from the Raksha's fallen victims.

Some of the soldiers wanted to retreat, while others such as Prime Shield Malik seemed poised to fight to the death. Surviving warriors from that battle all agree that the Prime Shield is what kept them all alive that long night. Malik kept the regiment together from the first assault of the Raksha, even as the creature's mighty swings felled dozens of men at a time. The power difference was stark, and the Shields' odds for victory seemed grim. At one point, the cackling monster announced himself to the audience, gleefully telling them his name was Obalu the Ravenous. And all he wanted was to feed on them. The Raksha was terrifying in every sense of the word, but the regiment knew that if they didn't defeat the nightmare creature, then his rampage would never end.

The Conflict

Some of the finest soldiers in the Holy Armada were picked for the critical and dangerous mission of combating Obalu. Any creature capable of effortlessly killing two Celestial Shields had to be taken seriously. The mission was marked as voluntary due to the nature of their enemy. A hunt of an unknown beast only had the highest chance of success when all their personnel wanted to be there. Even with extreme dangers, the Order had little trouble finding volunteers for this possible suicide mission.

The exact number of deployed soldiers is slightly disputed, as a regiment size can vary based on turnout. Ordinarily, a regiment of Divine Order soldiers is 1,800, though in this case, they had an increased number of volunteers. For this mission, estimates indicate between 1,800 to 2,000 troops from the Divine Order of the Phoenix marched toward the woods.

Battlefield

When the troops first set off for the unknown monster, they didn't know where the trail would ultimately lead them. They prepared for battle on a variety of terrains, be it the open field, forest, or caves. The final battle, however, took place in a small clearing outside the cave that had served as Obalu's nest. It was a dangerously cramped area to fight in, and the walking slaughterhouse that was the Raksha only made the staging arena that much smaller.

HAHAHA! YESSSS WELCOME, FLESHLINGS. I AM OBALU THE RAVENOUS HUNGER. YESSSS. IT'S A GOOD DAY TO FEAST, DON'T YOU THINK? HAHA AHAHAHA YESSSSS!!!!

— OBALU, HIS PROCLAMATION AS HE SQUARED UP AGAINST THE REGIMENT OF SOLDIERS

The Engagement

The battle against Obalu the Ravenous was one of almost sheer attrition. The behemoth's insane physical strength was daunting in the deepest of ways. Some of the warriors afterward remarked that they wondered if that's what it's like to fight a deity. Obalu could lash out with his stained spear and impale four to five people at a time. He was effortless in his carnage. No one could figure out where the spears came from either. Obalu seemed to pull them out of the ground and behind his back like deadly ethereal spears, yet the way they pierced men like paper showed they were more than just conjured weapons.

The battle went on for hours as waves of men met the reincarnated horror in battle, each soldier adding their mark, their slash, before retreating. With every leap into battle, they tested their luck against Xavian's chosen horror. Eventually, a soldier's luck ran out as a timed dodge was intercepted with a sharp thrust from a spectral spear. The fighting force had lost a third of its troops from this cycle of carnage repeating over a few hours. Obalu had started bleeding from the thousands of small cuts the regiment had rendered upon him. Yet through it all, the Raksha smiled and laughed with each blow to his massive frame.

It was when the Prime Shield Malik Faye started invoking the Pangool gods that the tide felt like it could turn. The veteran Shield had been measuring the monster, gauging when to use his limited powers. With the power of the Pangool shield gods, Malik weathered some of Obalu's heavy blows. This opportunity allowed more of the troops to focus on the tender, vulnerable parts of the thrashing daemon. Each life lost represented a small amount of the monster's health chipped away.

Malik cycled through the Pangool pantheon, unleashing a number of techniques including some that no one outside of The See'er Sigil Temples had seen. Watching a Prime Shield work their special brand of invocation was the awe-inspiring morale push the shrinking army needed. However, as the battle raged through the evening dusk and into the night, the Raksha clearly had the superior stamina, the sort of energy that only comes from a creature of another plane of existence. The Prime Shield Malik, a warrior with over 50 years of experience, made a desperate gambit for success.

While Kalali the East continues to be one of the most famous Prime Shields in the history of The Celestial Shields of the Eternal Flame, Malik is remembered as the bravest. Using himself as a trap and shield, the veteran warrior took a spear through his body but trapped Obalu's arm in his chest cavity before using an invocation to harden his skin and grip. With the mammoth horror immobilized, Malik gave the order for a last ditch, full-on assault. Sensing their chance, the remaining soldiers rushed in and hacked relentlessly at Obalu, pouring their all into their strikes.

Even with an arm trapped, the Raksha still killed a score of fighters as they stabbed and cut away at the nightmare creature. Finally, after a bloody fight that had lasted the better part of the late day and night, Obalu sank to his knees. The wicked grin never faded from his bloodstained face. Even in death, the Raksha mocked the living. The battleground served as the final resting place of Malik Faye, who expired shortly after Obalu's energy faded back toward the void. The Prime Shield himself smiled back at the nightmare creature, seemingly proud in humanity's effort. He is hailed as largely the reason the Celestial Shields even won the battle that day, and his name is still said with reverence in the Ilun Valley and Ghinor region.

Outcome

After a bloody 50-year reign, the mystery of Ghinor's massacre finally came to a close as Obalu was slain. However, the Celestial Shields paid a terrible cost in human lives for this victory. Many have questioned afterward if this horrific tragedy could have been averted if authorities had believed the initial survivors.

Aftermath

To this day, Ghinor remains a ghost town. Before the shadow of a Raksha stained their doorstep, the settlement had been a rising lumber town, though it and the general area now lies abandoned. The strength of the spirits in the area makes it uncomfortable for most humans to stay for extended periods.

Over the years, various Spirit Mediums have visited the area in an attempt to help ease the spirits of the area. After a few weeks, and sometimes even months, of effort, these Mediums all report the same thing: the area is too contaminated by the Raksha's murderous glee to connect with the ghosts. Over time, the residue from the otherworldly beast will fade, and perhaps the area can be smudged. As of the present, Ghinor remains a haunting tomb, a reminder of the power of a Raksha.

Historical Significance

Before the Massacre of Ghinor, the Raksha were simply bedtime stories that adults used to scare the pants off children. However, after the public as a whole began to learn the truth behind the Haunted Woods of Ghinor and the decimation of the town, that sentiment changed. When once the Karu would casually mention The Withering King Xavian by name, that all stopped after Ghinor.

The amount of bloodshed that happened at Ghinor made the threat of Xavian seem very real, and was taken seriously as such. Xavian's Touch, unfortunately, has also faced renewed scrutiny in the centuries after the incident. Previously considered a sort of rage disease, Xavian's Touch was now seen as a carrier for death. Discrimination and violence against those perceived to have the disease have skyrocketed.

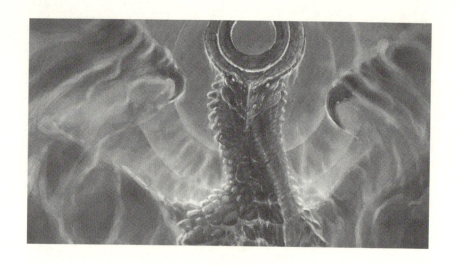

CHAPTER 7 | ADUME

Tikor sits under the watchful eyes of two suns. One built by the cosmos, the other a vile afterbirth.

Nestled on the horizon, Adume sits behind Tikor's first sun as one of the few things The Withering King ever created. The second sun of Tikor is said to be the fiery remains of the contemptible womb Xavian used to birth The Wretched Ones. Around the beginning of Tikor, the corruption god battled with the mother creator Ishvana. In a ploy she never thought possible, Xavian abducted a number of the planet's elemental spirits, creating a prison-like womb around them. What hatched were no longer her children, but horrifying world-breaking dragons.

In a twist of fate and perhaps luck, the dragon Ryuujin recollected his previous life as an Earth Elemental when he touched Tikor's soil. He escaped Xavian's mind control and helped turn the course of the battle. The remains of the prison that birthed the dragons, still smoldering with raw power, then became a second sun above the planet—an unwanted reminder of Xavian's influence and a source of unremitting heat for the southern half of Tikor.

Southern Discomfort

The original sun sits in its fixed point as Tikor and the other heavenly bodies revolve around it. The cursed sun Adume, however, doesn't seem to hold a fixed point, nor do other heavenly bodies seem to orbit it. As far as astrologers can tell, Adume maintains an orbit that keeps its rays directly on Vinyata.

It's estimated that the temperatures in the south would

be, on average, 35 degrees cooler if Adume was not present, which would have allowed the development of vegetation and other delicate life. The second sun has such a profound effect on the land that one could believe Vinyata was cursed if its progenitor, Ryuujin, had not handpicked the spot. The Dracon say it is to own a sense of his birth while the Karu say he chose the area out of atonement, though many people would think otherwise if they knew the true nature of Adume.

Strange Results

Around a decade before the world changing events of The Longest Night, Kent Musa and the Omicron Space Lab launched a surprise project under the cover of night. Using adapted missile technology, Musa and his team sent out a space probe. For quite some time, the pioneers at Omicron had gazed up at the sky and wondered what could be.

It took years for them to find a speed that allowed their probe to break the strange barrier around the atmosphere. With the adaptation of some Latimer drives, Musa's probe breached that barrier for a few seconds. The data that they received from this excursion caused the CEO to swear the entire team to secrecy. They pored over this data repeatedly to ensure the validity of their findings.

Kent and his team were floored by what they had discovered: Adume was not a sun. Xavian's creation didn't pulsate like the original, unnamed sun. Adume was darker, different. The core body itself couldn't be detected, only the edges. The "second sun" was a black hole.

Dark Edge Of Science

Many have wondered where the Divine Entities like Ishvana and Xavian came from. What created that which created us? This question is too large for most to ask, let alone answer. A crazy tale and theory has gone around for centuries, only believed by the most devout. The tale says that a man came across a puzzle box. Intrigued by the beauty of the box and detail of the puzzle, he set to open it. It took him a total of 15 years to solve the puzzle, but when he did, he found a head in the box. One of the fabled Godheads, it awoke and offered to answer any of his questions. The man asked where the greatest of them all, Ishvana, came from.

The head gazed deep into the man and whispered, "From a hole so dark that only light remains, a place not for the mortal coil. Pray until thy death that the door stays closed." The image of the door appeared in the man's mind, rendering him blind. Some believe this a cautionary tale about asking for too much. However, a fringe theory came from a quaint quip, "What if the gods came through a portal deep in space?" The theory usually devolved into the distance lizard people could travel, rendering it forgettable for most. What Musa found, however, put a light on that fringe theory.

The Womb's Collapse

Musa's team came up with a set of theoretical assumptions based on the brief burst of information they received and historical documents like the tale of the puzzle box. The star womb that Xavian created most likely did not begin as a sun. After The Wretched Ones were birthed from the celestial object, it collapsed upon itself. This event either created a black hole with the force of the collapse, or perhaps the black hole was at the center of the womb the whole time, and the collapse merely revealed its true nature. Either way, the end result was a black hole that began to emit enough light to change the surface temperature of Tikor. Thankfully, this second sun was far enough away to not destroy Tikor. Adume has always been a silent mystery in the sky, a source of many myths and tales. Omicron had accidentally stumbled across some answers to these tales, and even more mysteries.

Omicron has attempted to break through the atmospheric barrier to gather more data, but all subsequent efforts have failed. While no one on the probe team doubts the validity of their work or data, they are not ready to go public without the ability to verify their information. The news that the second sun is something more would be a lot to accept, and it raises far more questions than it answers. Until further evidence can be collected, Kent Musa has ordered the entire experiment to be kept top secret.

GLOSSARY OF MAJOR TERMS

Adume – The second sun within Tikor's solar system. It once was a womb for The Wretched Ones.

Beneath It All – A separation pocket dimension where Xavian is sealed.

Celestial Shield – Elite warriors of Garuda, trained by the See'er in ancient temples. They are considered the strongest fighters in the world.

Elementals – Ancient primal energies that were created along with the planet Tikor.

Ether – The name for the energy that powers all life.

Divine Entities – The name for the beings older than the planet Tikor itself. Gods of unknown and yet great power.

Divinity, The – The general name for all the deities of Garuda. Also the specific name for a group of the oldest and most revered of Garuda's deities.

Ether – The energy that flows through all life. If it's alive, it has Ether.

Etherforce – The name for the natural occurring flow of Ether.

Ishvana – An ancient creation god that is responsible for creating Tikor and much of its life; sacrificed herself to seal Xavian.

Garuda – The largest nation in the Northern Hemisphere; home to The Divinity and controlled by the Divine Order of the Phoenix.

Hekan - The name of magic in Tikor.

Omicron Technologies – The largest maker and develop of hekan based technology in the world.

Prime Shield – A title given the most senior and powerful of Celestial Shields.

Raksha – Ravenous monsters created by Xavian; sealed in Beneath It All.

Vinyata – The largest nation in the Southern Hemisphere. Home to The Four Pillars and controlled by The Republic of Vinyata.

Xavian – An ancient corruption god responsible for the corruption of the Elementals. Sealed away in Beneath It All.

Xavian's Touch – A cursed disease in which Xavian invades a human, slowly corrupting them until they give in and become a Raksha.

CHRONICLES OF TIKOR

A collection of lore and short stories from the Swordsfall Universe.

The Bank Heist: A Swordsfall Lore Book

Mustaf was having a normal day until the Killer Krew walked into his bank. The unofficial king of pirates, Nubia, is looking for something. And when she wants something, she gets it. Accompanied by her three Vice-Captains, the foursome are the most feared pirates on Tikor.

Will Mustaf survive this bank heist?

And what could the Killer Krew want in his bank?

Four Stages: A Swordsfall Lore Book

A Spirit Medium from an elite division known as The Eyes of Garuda was commissioned to help in the investigation of a grisly quadruple homicide. The investigators assigned were baffled by the case. What they uncovered during the Mediums vision would change everything.

This vision would give the first glimpse into Xavian's Touch, a deadly mixture of curse and disease that links the victim to The Withering King himself, Xavian.

The following is a re-telling of what the Medium saw that fateful day.

Volume 1: Tikor, The Beginning: A Swordsfall Lore Book

Tikor is a world where deities and spirits are as real as the nature that surrounds them.

Since the earliest writings of mankind, the gods have been there with them.

Swordsfall isn't just a story, it's a world. It's a dive into pre-colonial Africa for all the rich lore you've never heard of.

It's an exploration into a world where the majority of the faces are dark, yet isn't constrained to one corner.

It's a world where women hold power equal to men and the merit of one's soul is what propels them through life. It's a world where spirits aren't to be feared, they are to be embraced. In a time where we know that representation matters, this project is an effort to add to that spirit in the way I know best.

BOOKS BY THIS AUTHOR

The Summit Of Kings, Battle For The Supreme Jalen: A Swordsfall Rpg Adventure

The Summit of Kings is a 2 – 4 player one-shot set in the Swordsfall universe. It can be played in several different ways. You can play it as a fun one-shot with your group, or an amusing detour for the Jalen in your Swordsfall group. Or, with a bit of homebrewing, an adventure in your system of choice. Either way, the goal is to have a unique experience of a classic rap battle of your table.

The Summit Of Kings
Once a year there is a special, one of a kind tournament held on the beautiful coast of The Isle. The Summit of Kings. A yearly battle where the top Jalens from around the world are invited to find out who is the best in straight oratorial combat. The only way to get into the Summit is through a special invite. Regardless of how well you place at The Summit, just the act of receiving an invite is considered a prestigious honor. The worldwide Jalen organization, The Sixteen, keep track of the millions of wordsages around Tikor. When the list goes out, the people listen. So, after spending months powering through the tales, speeches, and recordings of current Jalens, the Hot List is formed. The tournament set.

Over 10,000 people flock to the private beach, Boogie Cove, and the town that surrounds it, South Onyx, to witness the awesome battle. The partially secluded vista is the perfect backdrop for the lyrical battle. Owned by the reclusive Grandmaster Jalen, Flayshe, it serves as a gorgeous backdrop for the lyrical tournament.

Who Will Be Crowned The Wordsmith?
The rules are simple. One on One, Jalen vs Jalen, Winner Takes All. Each Jalen takes there turn delivering the most crowd thrilling rap possible while the other patiently watches, careful to maintain a neutral face. They each vie for the roar of the crowd and the growing look of defeat on their foes face. Each summit battle lasts for three rounds with the winner being the best out of two.

Includes Character Sheets
Summit of Kings comes with it's own character sheets. And not just any, but the fancy kind. You can print them as normal or use your favorite PDF software to enter in the values on the sheet itself.

ABOUT THE AUTHOR

Brandon Dixon

Brandon lives in the Portland area of Oregon with his other half, Ashley. When he's not obsessed with Swordsfall, he works fruitlessly on completing his burgeoning Steam game library.

Connect with Swordsfall:

WEBSITE: swordsfall.com
PATREON: patreon.com/swordsfall
TWITTER: twitter.com/swordsfall1
FACEBOOK: facebook.com/swordsfallrpg
INSTAGRAM: instagram.com/swordsfallrpg

Made in the USA
Middletown, DE
08 November 2020